My Mom Made Me
Take Piano Lessons

MRS STODGE
PIANO LESSONS

A Doubleday Book for Young Readers
Published by Delacorte Press
Bantam Doubleday Dell Publishing Group, Inc.
1540 Broadway, New York, New York 10036
Doubleday and the portrayal of an anchor with a dolphin are trademarks of
Bantam Doubleday Dell Publishing Group, Inc.
Text copyright © 1994 by Judy Delton
Illustrations copyright © 1994 by Lisa McCue

Library of Congress Cataloging in Publication Data

Delton, Judy.
My mom made me take piano lessons / by Judy Delton ; pictures by Lisa McCue.
p.   cm.
Summary: Archie's complaints about his piano lessons cutting into
his playtime subside when his schoolteacher presents the
opportunity for Archie to become a star.
ISBN 0-385-31091-9
[1. Piano—Instruction and study—Fiction.] I. McCue, Lisa, ill. II. Title.
PZ7.D388Myp 1994   [E]—dc20   92-45661   CIP   AC

Manufactured in the United States of America

April 1994

10 9 8 7 6 5 4 3 2 1

To Tom, Ann, and Pam

And for Auntie Ree,
who was the piano player
in our family so long ago

My Mom Made Me Take Piano Lessons

by Judy Delton
pictures by Lisa McCue

A Doubleday Book for Young Readers

"There is a new piano teacher in town," said my mom, from behind the newspaper she was reading.

I kept watching TV.

"Wouldn't it be nice if you took lessons?" she said.
"You could play for Aunt Kate. And you could play at Christmas."

"Me?" I said. "Piano is for sissies. No guys I know play the piano."

"My cousin Willie played the piano," my mom went on. "He was in a recital in the town hall. The whole family came to hear him play."

"No way," I said. "I'm not taking piano lessons."

The next day my mom signed me up.

"I'm not going," I said.
"I have games to pitch.
A bike to ride.
I'll hit the wrong keys.
I'll lose my music book."

"You'll love it," said my mother. "You have the long fingers of a pianist, just like Cousin Willie."

The men delivered the used piano.

"Wrong house," I told them.

But my mom said, "Put it right here."

"It's too big," I said. "There's no room for the TV."

"The TV can go in the basement," said my mom.
She polished the piano with a spray that smelled like lemons.

I went outside and kicked a rock.
"I have to take piano lessons," I told my
friend Lars.

"I wouldn't take piano lessons," he said.
"Nobody could make me."

Thursday was my first lesson.
My teacher's name was Mrs. Stodge.
She had gold bracelets and blue hair.

"All the notes have names, Archie," she said to me. "This is middle C."

The first song had three notes. All three were middle C.
Anybody could play them. C C C. With one finger.

The song had no words. What good is a song with no words?
She made me play it over and over. My finger got stiff.

"You practice this song every day," she said. She pasted a red star on the page, and she gave me some lemonade.

"Practice?" I said.

When the lesson was over, I got out of there fast. I didn't even say good-bye. I didn't even thank her for the lemonade.

When I got home, I threw my music book on the piano.
I wanted to throw it in the wastebasket.

"How was the lesson?" asked my mom. "Was the teacher nice? Can you play a song?"

"I hate it," I said. "It's a dumb song. It has no words. I'm not going back."
"Give it time," said my mother. "Rome wasn't built in a day."

The next day my mom made me practice.
I had to sit and play the song with middle
C over and over. C C C. It hurt my ears.
My dog, Clyde, whined. It hurt his ears,
too.

"That's beautiful, Archie!" cooed my
mother.
She stopped doing dishes to listen.
"I love a house filled with music!" she said.

On Saturday Lars came over with his new
board game.
But I had to practice.
On Sunday Aunt Kate invited me to swim
in her pool.
But I had to practice.

On Monday I heard a fire engine. It went
right by my house.
But I couldn't follow it. I had to practice.
Just middle C. Over and over again.

On Thursday Mrs. Stodge said, "Wonderful! You are learning fast! Today we have a new song."

The new song had four notes.
C C and G G. With the same finger.
Didn't piano players have two hands?

Mrs. Stodge pasted a blue star on the page.
"Practice every day," she said.
Then she gave me a chocolate chip cookie and showed me her stamp collection. The cookie was good.

I played the new song at home. Clyde put his paws over his ears. He pretended he was scratching, but he didn't fool me.
My mom stopped painting to listen. "There's nothing like music to soothe the savage beast," she said.

The only beast I know around here is Clyde. And it didn't soothe him.

On Thursday Mrs. Stodge said, "I have a surprise! Today you will learn to play with two hands!"

I've had better surprises.
I played with two hands all right. One finger on each hand.

"You have such talent!" said my mother that night. She liked the two-hand song so much I played it again.
It was the least I could do.

After Labor Day school started.
"Now I'll have homework," I said to my mom. "I won't have time for piano."

"First things first," said my mom.

Piano got harder. Mrs. Stodge made me play three notes at the same time. It was called a chord.

I had to admit, a chord did sound fancy.

At school our teacher said, "This year we are going to have a little concert. Does anyone play an instrument?"
Lars was waving his hand. "Archie can play the piano!" he shouted.

"That's wonderful!" said the teacher. "Then Archie will be our star! The rest of you will play the triangles and bells."

She passed out triangles and bells to the other kids. Some had to hit little sticks against bent metal bars. The others shook bunches of bells tied to straps. But I was the only one who played real music. I was the star.

"When we get really good," the teacher said, "we can play on the stage. For the Christmas program."

The stage? I'd better tell Mrs. Stodge I have to learn "Jingle Bells"!

When I got home, my mom said, "I have been thinking about those piano lessons, Archie. I know you have homework. And you need time to play. Maybe you should quit piano until spring."

I thought about Mrs. Stodge's blue hair.
And the stars she gave out.
I thought about how everyone would admire me onstage.

"Quit?" I said. "I've got talent. Rome wasn't built in a day."

Wait till she sees me on that stage. Aunt Kate will be there, and all the relatives. Maybe even Cousin Willie. My name will be on the program. I'll probably have to take a bow.

I won't tell Mom about the Christmas program yet.
I'll save it for a surprise.

Judy Delton has written more than one hundred books for young readers, including two other stories featuring Archie, *My Mom Made Me Go to Camp* and *My Mom Made Me Go to School*, and the Dell Young Yearling books about the Pee Wee Scouts. She lives in St. Paul, Minnesota.

Lisa McCue has illustrated several books for children, including the My Mom books by Judy Delton. She lives in Bethlehem, Pennsylvania.